Dear Parent:
Your child's love of reading starts here!

Every child learns to read in a different way and at his or her own speed. Some go back and forth between reading levels and read favorite books again and again. Others read through each level in order. You can help your young reader improve and become more confident by encouraging his or her own interests and abilities. From books your child reads with you to the first books he or she reads alone, there are I Can Read Books for every stage of reading:

SHARED READING
Basic language, word repetition, and whimsical illustrations, ideal for sharing with your emergent reader

BEGINNING READING
Short sentences, familiar words, and simple concepts for children eager to read on their own

READING WITH HELP
Engaging stories, longer sentences, and language play for developing readers

READING ALONE
Complex plots, challenging vocabulary, and high-interest topics for the independent reader

ADVANCED READING
Short paragraphs, chapters, and exciting themes for the perfect bridge to chapter books

I Can Read Books have introduced children to the joy of reading since 1957. Featuring award-winning authors and illustrators and a fabulous cast of beloved characters, I Can Read Books set the standard for beginning readers.

A lifetime of discovery begins with the magical words "I Can Read!"

Visit www.icanread.com for information
on enriching your child's reading experience.

THE DARK KNIGHT RISES™

Batman versus Bane

Adapted by Jodi Huelin

Illustrated by Andie Tong

INSPIRED BY THE FILM THE DARK KNIGHT RISES
SCREENPLAY BY JONATHAN NOLAN AND CHRISTOPHER NOLAN
STORY BY CHRISTOPHER NOLAN AND DAVID S. GOYER
BATMAN CREATED BY BOB KANE

Sandy Creek

Sandy Creek
NEW YORK

An Imprint of Sterling Publishing
387 Park Avenue South
New York, NY 10016

For years, Gotham City
was an unsafe place.
Robberies were common.
Criminals ruled the streets.
Then came Batman.
He fought the crooks
and villains.
He used his brains and
gadgets to make
Gotham City safe.

Even the police relied on Batman.

Police Commissioner Gordon would shine

a special light into the sky

whenever he needed Batman's help.

Then, one day, Batman vanished.

Gotham's protector was gone.

There is a new villain in town.

His name is Bane.

His goal is to destroy

Gotham City.

The Gotham police are helpless.

Bane is too strong to stop

and too smart to catch.

To show how dangerous he is,
Bane kidnaps Commissioner Gordon
and holds him in his secret lair
deep in the underground tunnels.

When Bane is distracted,

Commissioner Gordon escapes.

Gordon races through the tunnels,

barely making it to safety.

Gordon is found by the police.

They take him to the hospital.

"You're back?" Gordon asks.

"Gotham needs me," Batman says.

Gordon tells Batman

where Bane is hiding.

Batman promises to find

this new foe and to stop him.

Batman zooms off on the Bat-Pod.

He meets Alfred back at the Batcave.

Together they form a plan.

With Alfred's help,

Batman prepares to take on Bane.

He downloads a map

of the underground tunnels.

He fills his belt with

weapons and gadgets.

He makes sure he's ready

for the battle to come.

GOTHAM SEWER MAP

Batman enters the tunnels.

He winds his way down into the darkness
and finds Bane's headquarters.

Batman watches as Bane and
his men discuss their latest crime.
Batman hides in the shadows,
waiting for his chance.

Finally, Bane's men leave.

Bane is all alone.

When he isn't looking,

Batman pounces.

But Bane is strong and fast.

He grabs Batman.

The two men wrestle and tumble.

The Dark Knight jumps to his feet

and lunges at the villain.

They fight and struggle.

Bane and Batman are equally matched.

Batman grabs Bane

and pushes him into the wall.

Bane breaks a pipe.

Water shoots at Batman!

The blast catches Batman off guard.

He doesn't see what happens next!

Bane uses the shadows against

his opponent and knocks Batman out.

After a while, Batman wakes up.

He's alone in a strange place.

There is no sign of Bane or his men.

Batman vows that this is not the end.

He will bring Bane to justice

and save Gotham City!